First hardcover edition October 2020

Book design and illustrations by Rebecca Caplinger

ISBN 978-1-0879-1366-7 (paperback)

# Dance with Lightning Bugs

WRITTEN BY ANNA CARTER
ILLUSTRATED BY REBECCA CAPLINGER

Lillian loved listening to Grandpa tell stories. They would sit on the porch and drink lemonade until dusk. Summer nights with Grandpa were her favorite.
They would catch lightning bugs and place them into jars while dancing around. She looked forward to the fireflies lighting up the jar and then releasing them.

"Lillian, it's time to go to bed. Go brush your teeth. I will be inside to tell you a story."

Grandpa tucked Lillian into bed.

"As time passes I am getting older and weaker. You are special to me. I have a story written specifically for you."

"What is the story about grandpa?"

"This story is about you silly girl. I may not always be around to tell you." Grandpa was sad. He had a tear roll down his cheek.

"My dear child as you snuggle in your bed and soon fall asleep, let me share with you why my love for you is so deep."

I hoped for a masterpiece when I was waiting for you.
You surpassed my imagination so wild of a view.

You were made unique from the start.
Be proud of your gifts, setting you apart.

I hope that you will grow up strong and confident like a tree. Please know that you can become whomever you are called to be.

I want you to look fear in the eye, go on, give it a try!

Chase dreams up high to the mountain top and even the sky.

May you laugh with gorillas at the zoo.
Remember to always say thank you and
God bless you after achoo!

Laugh on a rollercoaster
when you reach up high.
Run in the ocean
at low tide.

Fall in love so deep and wide.
Take new adventures like a
hot air balloon ride.

Dance with lightning bugs on the
fourth of July and paint on a
canvas of a moon lit sky.

Remember that life is good and to
enjoy each day. You are beautiful
in every way.

Always know that thoughts become wishes and wishes become dreams. You can be anything if you only believe.

Lillian fell fast asleep. Grandpa went outside to admire the night sky. He was amazed as he saw thousands of lightning bugs light up the sky. He grabbed his cane and decided to dance with the lightning bugs one last time.